Where, Oh Where, Is Santa Claus?

Where, Oh Where,

Scholastic Inc.

New York Toronto London Auckland Sydney

Mexico City New Delhi Hong Kong Buenos Aires

Is Santa Claus?

Written by
Lisa Wheeler

Illustrated by
Ivan Bates

ISBN-13: 978-0-545-03636-8
ISBN-10: 0-545-03636-4

Text copyright © 2007 by Lisa Wheeler.
Illustrations copyright © 2007 by Ivan Bates. All rights reserved.
Published by Scholastic Inc., 557 Broadway, New York, NY 10012,
by arrangement with Houghton Mifflin Harcourt Publishing Company.
SCHOLASTIC and associated logos are trademarks and/or registered
trademarks of Scholastic Inc.

12 11 10 9 8 7 6 5   9 10 11 12 13/0

Printed in the U.S.A.   08

First Scholastic paperback printing, November 2008

In memory of
Grandpa Oren and Grandma Margaret Wheeler,
who made every day like Christmas
—L. W.

For Lucas and Clara
—I. B.

Stamping-tramping
reindeer feet
clomp and stomp through
polar sleet.

Step-by-step in
Christmas snow,
search for Santa.
Where'd he go?

Clip-clop, clip-clop, two-by-two.
Santa! Santa! Where are you?

Fuzzy-furry
polar ears
hear the hooves of
Santa's deer.

Whiskers twitching
in the snow.
Hurry, bunnies—
off you go!

Hip-hop, hip-hop, polar paws.
Where, oh where, is Santa Claus?

Harking-barking
seal-pup twins
coast along on
polar fins.

Flippers flopping.
Bellies glide.
Follow bunnies.
Slip and slide.

Flip-flop, flip-flop, polar two.
Santa! Santa! Where are you?

Swishing-swooshing
polar tail.
Pit-pat paws go
down the trail.

Trekking-tracking
foxy nose.
Sniffs for Santa—
off she goes!

Pit-pat, pit-pat, polar paws.
Where, oh where, is Santa Claus?

Bumbling-tumbling
polar cub
toddles from
his arctic tub.

Icy droplets
splash and spray.
Shake, shake, shake—
he's on his way!

Thump-bump, thump-bump, polar paws.
Where, oh where, is Santa Claus?

Ziggy-zaggy
tricky track.
Crisscross, crisscross,
doubles back.

Giant paws
in snowy drifts ...
Who has left
these polar prints?

Flicking-kicking
funny feet.
Upside down
in polar sleet.

Stumble-fumble
in the snow.
Snowshoes wagging
to and fro.

Hurry-scurry, polar paws.
Rescue dear old Santa Claus!

Heave-Ho!

Heave-Ho!

Heave...

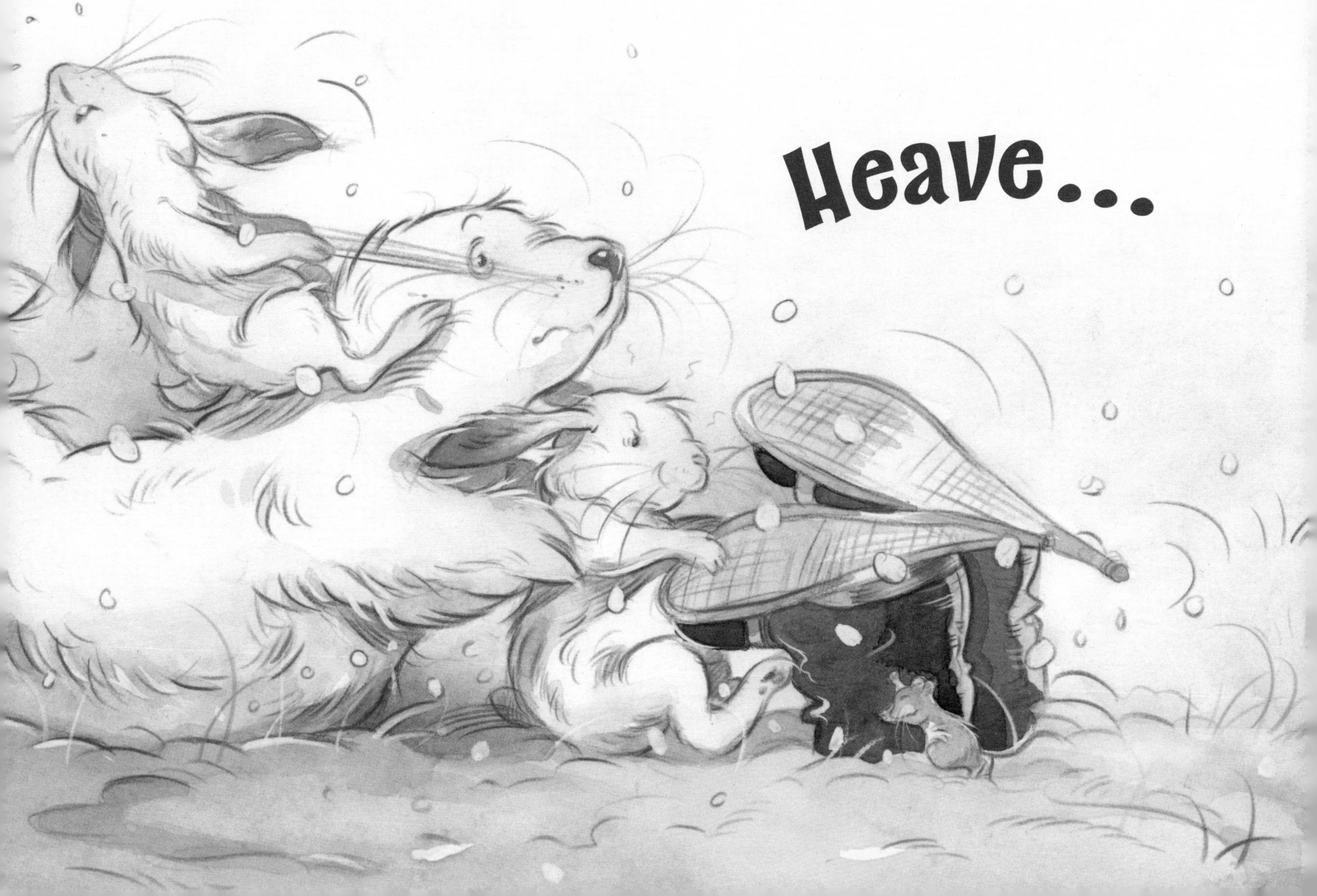

"Ho-Ho-Ho!"
says Santa Claus.
"Thank you, thank you,
polar paws!"

"Hurry, reindeer—
to the sleigh!"

Clip-clop, clip-clop . . .

The illustrations in this book were done in wax crayons
and watercolor on Fabriano Artistico paper.
The display type was set in Melanie.
The text type was set in Pumpkin and Catseye Bold.
Designed by Lydia D'moch